Angela J Kecojevic

Illustrated by Lyn Stone

HOBBLEDOWN

First published in Great Britain by Hobbledown Limited 2012

A CIP catalogue record for this title is available from the British Library
ISBN 978-0-9573145-0-4 (Hardback)
ISBN 978-0-9573145-1-1(Paperback)

Written by Angela J Kecojevic
Illustrated by Lyn Stone
Designed by Georgina Pensri

Acknowledgements

For Alex, Dimitri, Daniela and Anouska who have listened patiently to my lengthy ponderings about whatnots and thingamajigs.

To chief Hobblers, Richard Farley and Nick de Candole for letting me into their mysterical world of Hobbledown.

For their patience and support the chief Hobblers would like to thank their Hobblehagged wives and demanding Hobblings, Amelia, Vanessa, Ollie, Ben, Jaime and Maddie. To Angela and Lyn, a big special thanks. Not too torturous I hope. And to all the other Hobbledown book helpers, Mike, Schultz and Georgina.

Hobbledown exists! We would love to see you.

www.hobbledown.com

Down, down, down beneath the gumblegook trees
live the Hobblers of Hobbledown who speak Potenese.
As the moon shines bright over rooftops and dales,
the flags of Hobbledown soar and sail.
A snuffler snorts, a young bobilly bleats
as the tired animals prepare for their sleep.

A sleep full of mysterical magic and dreams
for Hobbledown is sometimes not quite as it seems.
Near the willows and woebegones is the muddlesome maze,
for confusion and adventure on warm summer days.
A jumble of paths leading this way and that
(or even that way and this) –
most certainly an adventure not to be missed.

Beyond the cobble-roof village is the Rumpletump's lair,

a thicket of trees called the Copse – BEWARE! – a place

where a scaly beast stomps and scares

the squawking gumblegooks up, up in the air.

Yet deep in the woodland where the fairy mounds grow,

is a secret door where the Hobblers go

to the Valley of Potenesia, a place once called home.

Where candy canes glisten on lemon-drop trees

and soft, pastel bubbles float and pop in the breeze.

Until one fine day when the Hobblers discovered

a place more magical than any other. A world full of

wonder, excitement and play where in harmony together

they could spend their days

in the Hobbledown mines, digging for magical stones

to keep stomp, stomping Rumpletump tucked up safe in

his home.

Yet apart from the Hobblers and animals you meet,
there is delightful Sludgebucket who muddles his
speech with nonsense, riddles, and hilarious rhymes
that will delight and amuse you time after time.
At the heart of Hobbledown stands the Quercus tree,
home to red-capped Fern, a Grig fairy
who merrily flits around fields and barns,
delighting the Hobblers with her mischievous charm.

Until its time for bed or a sweet piece of corn,
until the nodding bluebell chimes her nightime yawn
then a hush will fall across the twilight sky
and nature shall sing a soft lullaby; Fern then draws
her curtains and puts out the light
over mysterical Hobbledown where all now sleep tight.
Goodnight.

A little explanation . . .

Snuffler
Squiggly-tailed pig that is very fond of mud and apples.

Bobilly
Bearded goat with excellent climbing skills.

Grimwoolly
Woolly-haired sheep that loves lazy, grazing days and field racing.

Brayer
Rather stubborn long-eared donkey. Enjoys peppermints.

Pimpertail
Emerald-crested peacock with a glorious fan of fancy feathers.

Bomjad
Cottontail rabbit. Always in a hurry.

Gumblegook
Cackling and colourful bird that lives in the gumblegook trees.

Grig
British Grig fairy. These red-capped folk are usually found in meadows or near bluebells.

Noggin

One noggin is the same size as one human foot size. It is also the word for a Hobbler foot.

Quercus Oak

The oak is a member of a tree family called the Quercus. It grows acorns and is home to Hobbledown's resident fairy, Fern.

Skibblers

Mischievous creatures from the faraway Bogs of Skelactor.

Glime

A green slimy substance belonging to the Skibblers.

Willows and Woebegones

A deep pond set amongst willow trees with a secret path running to Hobbledown Village.

Field of Confusion

A muddlesome maze of willow.

Potenesia

A land where the Hobblers once lived. The language spoken by the Hobblers is Potenesian.

Rumpletump

A komodo-type dragon that lives in the Copse. He stomps a lot and is very happy eating custard pies.

Beginning...

... to end

The Book of Thingamajigs and Whatnots

There are two very important things you should know about Skibblers. First, if your eyes begin to water and your nostrils start to twitch then there is a very good chance that you are standing as close to a Skibbler as you should dare. Second, if you happen upon a trail of foul-smelling slime then do not even think to touch it. Absolutely and definitely not.

Skibbler slime is a thick and green substance that stinks like the breath of a Cachoocha hyena (frightful creatures who chew on eggs all day ... not for the faint-hearted). This slime will burp and spit a smelly vile spray over you that is dreadfully hard to clean off.

Third, (yes, I had forgotten one very important fact) you must blow your whistle and run as fast as your young or old legs will carry you. Not a 'running-for-the-bus' kind of pace, but a 'lion-is-chasing-you' kind of pace.

However, rarely has a Skibbler ever been sighted outside of the Bogs of Skelactus, therefore you should not be overly worried at the idea of meeting one. Although, in the same way that you or I would shiver (and scream) at finding a spider or a mouse in our kitchen cupboards, the discovery of a Skibbler would be very serious indeed. As serious as finding a womblebat in your cereal box or a crawlybug in your milkshake.

Something Unpleasant

Huck took a deep breath as he prepared to climb down the Quercus Oak. Climbing up had been easy yet as he began the journey back down to the tree's bulging roots, he knew one thing for certain – tree tops and darkness did not mix well when you were a Hobbler of only three noggins high. Huck stared up at the shimmering moon now lighting the sky over Hobbledown, and wondered how far away its silvery surface really was. It looked almost close enough to touch – much closer than the top of the tree to the ground below he thought gloomily.

Halfway up the Quercus, tucked amongst the leaves, sat a small, wooden tree house topped with moss. By the front door a purple flag fluttered in the breeze – a flag that only flew when Fern, a Grig fairy, was at home and the only reason why Huck had decided to climb the tree – although maybe the thought of a piece of homemade pie had helped a little. To find neither had been rather worrying and quite disappointing.

Ignoring the sudden arrival of hiccups he always had when he was nervous, Huck threw his backpack to the ground — thud — and began to climb down, carefully holding onto the branches as he went. He didn't enjoy clambering around unbooted yet that very morning his gumboots had vanished and as Huck was the owner of two completely different sized noggins, it was baffling.

Down

      down

            down

       and

                  down

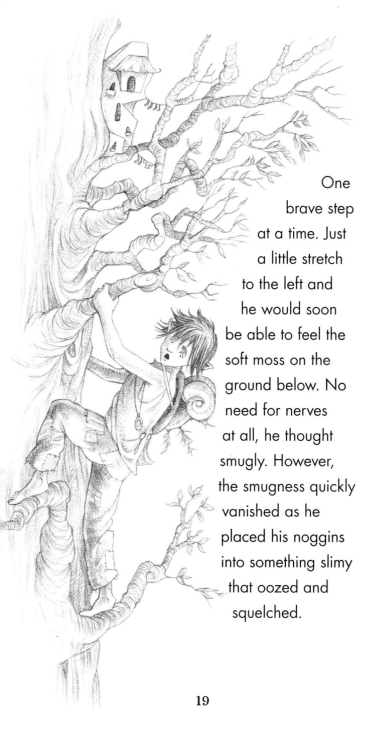

One
brave step
at a time. Just
a little stretch
to the left and
he would soon
be able to feel the
soft moss on the
ground below. No
need for nerves
at all, he thought
smugly. However,
the smugness quickly
vanished as he
placed his noggins
into something slimy
that oozed and
squelched.

Huck's eyes began to water, and his nose began to twitch – first left then right – as the pongiest smell he had ever smelt wafted up over him. He realised, as he pulled and twisted, that he was well and truly stuck. He tugged first with one leg and then with the other but the gooey stuff just gripped him tighter, spitting and spewing vile green bubbles.

The bubbles grew and grew and grew and as they grew, they made a sound that would scare the mightiest of Hobblers. For not only did they burp and bulge but also they belched and blew, giving poor Huck a dreadful fright.

'What is going on?' he muttered crossly, his hiccups now so humongous that he shook with every hic and jumped with every cup. He removed a whistle from around his neck, a whistle used in emergencies only, and right now, he considered his situation far greater than that – it was a catastrophe of Hobbler-sized proportions!

He needed to call upon the Hobblers as

fast as he could. (Hobblers came in all shapes and sizes – tall, short, thin and round, not forgetting the occasional giant-sized one that lived in eastern Potenesia.)

'Now, if I can just remember the right tune,' he said as he held the whistle to his lips. He puffed up his cheeks and blew into it, very long and very hard.

Not a sound came out. Not a single toot.

He tried again, this time blowing even harder.

The whistle spluttered and coughed then

out popped a melody of musical notes.

Notes that rose up into the night air then dashed off across the Willows and Woebegones, down through the Hobbledown mine and up over the Rickety Rack until they reached the cobble-roofed huts that belonged to the Hobblers; homes made of knotted wood and spindles and a silver walkway that shimmered in the moonlight. Hobblers were skilled carpenters and their homes were very mysterical indeed.

The notes floated down and vanished through the smoking chimney pot of one such home where Huck, Tipp and Eliza lived. First there was a clatter, and then a twang as two Hobblers received a very urgent and noisy message. Every Hobbler carried a whistle that could play bird tunes and hopefully, the high-pitched tune of a gumblegook would lead the Hobblers to Huck and help him get out of this terrible fix.

Back beneath the Quercus, Huck waited patiently to be rescued. If the quivering notes had taken a wrong turn, especially near the Willow Field of Confusion, then they could have been chewed alive by the only resident of the Copse – a terrible and grizzly end for any living or musical thing.

Rescue. Such an adventurous word Huck decided as he imagined himself bravely saving the Minister of Potenesia from one of the ghastly trolls that roamed in faraway Nevereverdom, not a word for someone stuck beneath an oak tree covered in something sticky.

'Huck, where are you?' came two voices belonging to Tipp and Eliza.

'I'm here,' replied Huck wiping away another blob of glime from his cheeks. 'What took you so long?'

'Your notes made quite a noise,' laughed Tipp. 'I was having a nap.'

Tipp was a little smaller than Huck and boasted a mop of bright red hair, which matched the spotted neckerchief he always wore. He grinned at the sight of his friend, ankle deep in goo whilst behind him, hurried

Eliza – rosy-cheeked with a tumble of curls pinned up beneath several pimpertail feathers.

'It looks like you've got yourself into quite a mess this time. I've never seen any glime like that around Hobbledown before,' she said, emptying the contents of her bag onto the ground – a mixture of test tubes and pots.

Tipp knelt down to take a closer look. He did not expect the sudden belch that erupted, covering his startled face with yucky, green spots. Tipp squealed louder than a baby snuffler and scurried backwards towards the safety of a nervous weeping willow.

'Not so funny now, is it?' said Huck in fits of laughter as Tipp scowled.

Eliza carefully removed the lid from a bottle containing a ruby liquid, placed a pair of goggles over her eyes and added a plastic cap to her hair. She was extraordinarily well prepared, thought Huck. Which could only mean one thing – mess!

He began to fidget nervously. 'Can you hurry? I'm not sure if I can stay upright any longer.'

'Eliza?' said Tipp. 'You're not going to do what I think you are going to do?'

'Well, I'm only doing what Professor Topperpot suggested to do if we ever got stuck in honey sap. Popping is the only solution,' Eliza replied defensively.

Huck glared at his friends. 'Popping sap is one thing but popping a strange green substance whilst I'm still standing in it is quite another.'

Eliza sighed impatiently. 'Ready?' she asked.

'Not really,' Huck grumbled as Eliza poured the liquid onto the glime then ran to

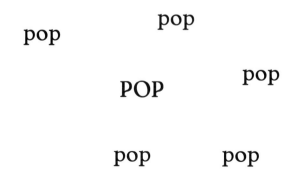

wait with Tipp behind the willow.

The sound echoed across Hobbledown as clouds of billowing green smoke puffed up into the air.

Huck didn't hear the giggling that came from behind the tree nor could he see the tears of laughter that poured down his friends' faces. He had been popped into the air like a bad-tempered cork and now hung from a branch upside down!

Silence followed. Not a gumblegook tweeted nor a daffer quacked. Even the woodentop reindeers stopped fighting. As the smoke drifted away, the two friends helped a very cross Huck down from the oak tree.

'Think you need a bath, Huck,' said Eliza, wiping her eyes dry.

'Eliza can add one of her special potions,' laughed Tipp.

'Have your fun,' said Huck, removing a lump of glime from his nose. 'I only climbed up to visit Fern … not to get into such a ridiculous fix. The whole thing is quite mysterical.'

Eliza wiggled a test tube containing a bubbling sample of glime. 'Don't worry. I'll take this to Professor Topperpot. Maybe he'll know what it is.'

Tipp, struggling to control his laughter, clapped Huck firmly on the back. 'Cheer up. It could have been worse. If the tune hadn't arrived on time, you'd be up to your neck in the stuff by now.'

Huck managed a slight smile. 'I guess so. We just need to find out how it got here and how to get rid of this dreadful smell.'

Eliza wrinkled her nose in disgust.

'I guess I do need a bath,' Huck said managing a slight grin. 'Come on. Last one home is a gumblegook!'

Off they went through the Willows and Woebegones with Huck leaving an incredibly slimy and thick trail behind him. A gooey trail that was about to bring a whole heap of trouble upon Hobbledown.

Rumpletump and Roses

An early morning lark snagged a dozing worm as wheelbarrows full of fresh hay and seeds were trundled towards the animals just in time for breakfast. The bobillies jumped merrily from bale to bale whilst the daffers waddled, two by two, towards the pond ready for their morning dip.

Yet, it wasn't just the animals preparing for a wash. Poor Huck was up to his neck in a wooden barrel overflowing with bubbles and flowers – something he was *not* enjoying. The splashing turned to spluttering as Tipp emptied an entire bottle of Eliza's rose-petal perfume into the foaming water, ignoring the terrible fuss that Huck was now making.

'Isn't that better?' Eliza called out from her window. 'That will get you smelling all flowery.'

'I don't want to smell flowery, thank you. I smell worse now than I did before,' said Huck furiously. 'I did say just two drops of perfume.'

Tipp chuckled and threw Huck a towel. 'You'd better hurry up otherwise once the bees set off on their honeyround they may decide to stop off at you first. Roses are their favourite.'

Huck climbed out, his head topped with flowers and looking very grumpy indeed. Bath time had not been fun.

Over near the snufflers, a group of elders sat sipping rosehip tea, watching the hustle and bustle around them as the Hobblers worked and played.

Professor Topperpot held weekly classes on animal care, a subject he considered extremely important for every Hobbler. The Professor taught them that looking after the snufflers and grimwoollies – in fact, all the animals on the farm, was a huge responsibility and every Hobbler would need to pass a test in order to be awarded the golden Hobbledown buckle.

A group of young Hobblers arrived, eager to learn about gumblegook care. They quickly sat down as the Professor produced a tub of worms and a cackling feathered animal that began pecking at the poor Professor's top hat!

Eliza was now tending the Hobblepatch whilst a much cleaner Huck scattered fresh corn and dandelion tops for Porello, Hobbledown's emerald-feathered pimpertail.

'Professor Topperpot has called for a meeting tonight,' said Huck. 'Let's hope we can find out what's going on.'

'I really hope so,' Eliza replied. 'The animals seemed unsettled this morning, especially the grimwoollies. Even Rumpletump was unusually noisy!'

'Rumpletump is always noisy,' Huck laughed, carefully sidestepping a beady-eyed Porello. 'I remember when he first arrived through the doorway from Potenesia as nothing bigger than a tiny rumple.'

'I remember too,' Eliza said fondly, 'and we used to ride about on his back but he grew so big, we couldn't climb up on him anymore. The Copse is a brilliant home for him and the crystallite barrier keeps him safely snug inside, otherwise he would have trampled on top of all of us by now. All the while the crystals are in place, we've nothing to worry about. Let him stomp as much as he likes!'

Eliza carried on digging deep grooves into the earth, carefully sewing a small handful of seeds into the soil, finishing off with a sprinkle of water. Above her head hung a sign.

Hobblepatch

A small patch of earth where the Hobblers could look after their vegetables and flowers. Sunflowers stood to attention above a cluster of tomato plants and flowering sweet peas whilst around the edges lay sprigs of basil, perfect for keeping unwanted bugs away.

'Oh no!' Huck cried, landing on the floor for the umpteenth time. Porello squawked, angrily flapping his feathers as Huck tried to shoo him up the wooden ramp where a tasty feast of fresh fruit and mealworms awaited. Porello was king of the birds and did not like being hurried.

'Eliza, give me a hand, he never usually makes this much fuss.'

'Maybe it's the smell of roses,' laughed Eliza as together they chased after Porello, flapping and shooing until he was back inside his home.

Huck removed a stray green and blue feather, caught on the horn of his hat and tucked it into Eliza's hair.

'There. A pimpertailed Eliza!' he laughed. 'It even matches your necklace.'

Eliza fiddled with the pale crystal that hung around her neck, a piece of crystallite that all the Hobblers wore. 'Not any more. It isn't the bright blue it usually is. It's slightly paler.'

'Let's hope nothing is wrong otherwise without the crystals' power, Rumpletump will be able to roam all over Hobbledown,' said Huck, sweeping up the last strands of straw 'and that would cause chaos!' He closed the gate as Porello strutted back out from his roost looking quite ruffled.

'Nearly finished,' said Eliza. 'Next stop

is Albert with this bag of tasty apple treats. I just hope he doesn't spit whilst I'm in there.' (A ghastly habit even for a llama.)

'I'm afraid I shall need to give him a miss today. I'm off to Potenesia to borrow the Book of Thingamajigs and Whatnots. After Professor Topperpot heard about my little … erm … fix yesterday, he thought it would be a good idea if I fetched over the old book. It has everything in it about creatures and lost treasures from all over the world, and hopefully it will have something about this stuff I stepped in.'

'The Professor took a look at the sample I collected but he'd never seen it before either,' said Eliza, heading off across Hobbledown. 'See you later.'

Huck brushed off the mud from his trousers and trudged down the path as the sun shone brightly overhead. He soon came to a wooden sign and the words …

The Willow Field of Confusion

Leaning against the sign was a smiley-faced Hobbler, wearing one of Professor Topperpots old top hats and a black bow tie. Only a smidgen of straw poking from his shirt cuffs revealed that this 'Hobbler' was in fact a scarecrow of the very smartest kind.

'Morning Mr Wobble … err … Mr Wimble,' Huck said creeping nervously around the straw man.

Mr Wimble stood next to the Willow Field of Confusion, a muddlesome maze right beside Rumpletump's home. Not only did the maze sprout the odd ear of corn responsible for Tipp's glorious corn and custard pie, but also in the unlikely event of Rumpletump venturing out, the scaly beast would be quite lost and very confused.

Mr Wimble shuddered as a gumblegook flew down and pecked him rather rudely on his nose. Unfortunately, Mr Wimble just happened to be a scarecrow that was not very good at scaring!

With no time to waste, Huck carried on until he came to another signpost.

THE COPSE
Camouflage recommended
Passageway to Potenesia
Beware of Rumpletump!

Huck could never quite understand why the last sentence was not in large glaring letters. He stood in front of the Copse, a thicket protected by glittering pieces of crystallite, and began covering himself from head to noggin in twigs and leaves, finishing off with a thick dollop of mud smeared across his face.

'Right, quick march. No time to think so no time to worry,' he muttered as he climbed through a gap in the fence, a gap designed for a very small Hobbler. He was nearly through when suddenly he found he could move no further. His satchel snagged on a thorny bush and for the second time in two days, he was terribly stuck. Huck wriggled to the left then wriggled to the right – he groaned and grunted until he could wriggle no more. He was exhausted.

Then he heard an oh-so familiar sound.

Swish, stomp, swish, stomp, swish, stomp. Huck froze. (Remember, when terribly stuck and a very large creature is approaching you must not panic, unless of course it is Rumpletump.) The gumblegooks, startled by such a noise, leapt cackling into the air. Huck's eyes widened as out of the bush came one giant claw followed by another.

Stomp, stomp, stomp.

A dragon-like creature appeared with bulging eyes and flaring nostrils that sniffed in search of intruders. Intruders like Huck.

Rumpletump stomped towards the fence, a stomping that shook the very roots of Hobbledown.

'Oh no … this is not good,' Huck said as he turned a peculiar shade of green. 'How do I get into such muddles?'

As a baby, Rumpletump had always been good-natured (well, as good-natured as any tiny rumple can be) but right now, at twenty noggins long, he was very bad tempered indeed. From his jaws dribbled a delightful measure of drool that slid down Huck's brown, tufty hair.

'Oh my goodness,' Huck whispered, for he was now quite frightened as any Hobbler ought to be when stuck in such an unpleasant and gooey situation.

Yet his fear turned to surprise as Rumpletump began to snort, then cough and finally splutter, and when a Rumpletump splutters you really should not be too close. With a tremendous sneeze, he thundered back into the bushes, winding his tail behind him in a serpent-like fashion.

Huck was speechless. It seemed the beast didn't like flowery smells either. Perhaps Eliza's rose potions had been a good thing after all.

Huck breathed in as hard as he could, digging frantically at the mud and roots around him until he'd made a little more room, and just when he thought he could do no more, his satchel loosened and out he popped.

Ahead were the silver birch trees and the door that separated Hobbledown from Potenesia. Like a freshly lit cannonball, he ran as fast as he could and fired himself through the small wooden door...

A Mysterical Day

Round and round Huck spun, firmly seated on top of his satchel, bumping down a narrow tunnel that twisted and dipped faster than a helter-skelter. (Underground journeys can often be very unpleasant.) Huck glanced up and saw a familiar sign …

Welcome to Potenesia

The satchel came to an abrupt stop, flinging Huck forward through a Hobbler-sized hole, straight out into the land of Potenesia.

A clock chimed and a cuckoo sang, as Huck found himself facing an odd-whiskered man wearing a patchwork coat and holding an unusually large fob watch.

'Hi, old Pip,' said Huck fondly.

'Welcome, Huck. You are exactly on time,' said the whiskery man with a smile. Old Pip *was* old (rumours of well over a hundred and fourteen) and as the Gatekeeper, he controlled all the doors that led into Potenesia. He locked the door behind them, returning the key carefully back amongst the others as each key belonged to one of the lands leading into Potenesia, Endlesdom, Hobbledown and even one named Nonsuch, and it was important that as the Gatekeeper, he kept an eye on all comings and goings.

'Must lock the door properly each time otherwise who knows what might try and creep through,' he said. 'Ruben reckons he heard a scratching and tapping noise beneath the cabin several days ago. It didn't sound like anything he'd ever heard before. Whatever they were, they must have made quite a noise to wake up sleepy Ruben!'

Old Pip looked at his watch impatiently. Another visitor was due at any second. Huck booked his return journey for exactly three hours' time and leaving behind the doorway to Hobbledown, he hurried along a passageway lined with pink-headed dandelions that roared proudly as the dainty primroses sighed and tittered.

At the end of the path was a small market square bustling with Hobblers, Potenesians, and even a few visitors from Nonsuch.

Huck stopped first at Humbugs, a shop made entirely of sugar cane and brimming with every sweet imaginable. Inside, burp-blasting whistles and chocolate covered dewdrops were bought using trogs, Potenesian coins.

A toad-like belch startled Huck, and he jumped, knocking over several boxes of wriggling jelly worms that slithered off causing chaos amongst the shrieking shoppers.

'Pesky wrigglers,' grumbled Mr Humbug as he chased after them with a small wicker basket.

'Erm … best be off,' muttered Huck as he hurried out to the next shop – Merrymakers Merry Box.

Merrymakers was a toyshop and as busy and merry as one would expect. A rumple-in-the box sprung up from the floor, startling several

tired mothers, waiting patiently whilst their young ones bought puppets, kaleidoscopes and all sorts of wonderful delights.

'Attention! Quick march,' cried an army of tin soldiers that marched up and down the middle of the shop whilst Huck darted about trying desperately to avoid them.

'Sorry … ouch … hooray!' he said as they strode across his noggins and off towards a smouldering miniature volcano.

'Target ahead. Quick march!' boomed a red-faced sergeant.

Laughter rang out as the amazing Potenesian kookaburras began their noisy mid-morning choir practice. It was quite clear that *anything* was possible at Merrymakers.

Huck hurried back out into the square, clutching a bag of Merrymakers' goodies. Set back amongst the trees a wooden shack towered high into the sky – Ruben's Cabin. As he pushed open the door, a bell clanged and a foghorn blasted a cool foggy cloud into the room. Owned by Ruben, one of Potenesia's

oldest residents, the Cabin was a treasure trove of the strangest kind, full of boxes and sacks bulging with anything and everything. Against wooden panelled walls, ladders rose higgledy-piggledy up towards the roof, up and up until Huck's eyes could see no further.

Professor Topperpot had assured him that the book lay tucked away on the fifteenth floor and as Huck began to climb one of the rickety ladders, he hoped that he would find exactly what he wanted *and* quickly. It was a little dark and creepy inside and Huck felt a small tremor of hiccups bubbling in his tummy, ready to surface at any second. As he reached the top rung, Huck discovered something he had not quite expected, and something that felt the force of his sudden and very loud hiccups. Ruben.

Now, Huck had heard stories of sleepy Ruben and his mysterical nose, yet standing face to face, Huck realised that he was gaping at the reddest, most enormous nose he had ever, **ever** seen. Gaping is never a polite thing

to do, *whatever* the condition and even if it *is* very large and bulbous.

Dressed in striped pyjamas and holding a lantern, white-bearded Ruben seemed to sway from side to side as if he was about to nod off.

'I usually sleep all day long for I live a

rather nocturnal life, like some of your animals I should imagine,' said Ruben stifling a yawn. 'Too much excitement and bustle, especially from Merrymakers, does *not* give me pleasant dreams. However, anyone in search of the Book of Thingamajigs and Whatnots must be in need of help, so awake I must be. The book is very special, young Hobbler and will not open unless it wants to.'

Huck stopped staring and rubbed at his eyes. Rubens swaying was making him feel sleepy too.

'Erm, how did you know I wanted the book?'

'The ancient book *knew* it was needed. It packed and labelled itself early this morning,' said Ruben turning towards an old bookcase. Huck could hear chattering and squabbling as from out of the shelf wriggled a large book wrapped in brown paper upon which the word *Hobbledown* was scribbled.

'It made an awful racket. I couldn't sleep a wink,' said Ruben yawning. 'Never mind, plenty of time to rest once I find out where that strange smell of roses is coming from. It will keep me awake for days!'

Huck turned an even deeper shade of red than Ruben's nose! The sooner he got back to Hobbledown the better. He mumbled his goodbyes and with the Book of Whatnots and Thingamajigs tucked safely inside his satchel, Huck hurried back towards the Gatekeeper, narrowly avoiding the snapping teeth of the dandelions, and perfectly on time for his slide back to Hobbledown.

Kaleidoscope

A fine mist floated down over the Copse as the door leading from Potenesia to Hobbledown slowly opened. Huck poked his head out and checked for Rumpletump. Beside the doorway, nestled in a ditch filled with bracken and leaves, Huck saw the gentle movement of a tail accompanied by a soft rumbling noise. He grinned. Rumpletump was fast asleep!

Huck stumbled over roots and stumps as he ran through the Copse until he reached the Willow Field of Confusion and the welcome sight of home. It was good to be back in Hobbledown.

'Hey, how was it?' asked Eliza, leaning

against a hay bale.

'Well, apart from having Rumpletump slobber over me, all things considered? Not too bad. Thanks to your roses, Eliza, I managed to scare off Rumpletump *and* leave poor Ruben unable to sleep. It was quite a day.'

See? I did help you after all,' giggled Eliza, swinging a coloured bag across her shoulders. 'Did you get the book?'

Huck held up a large brown package. 'Yes, it was all ready and waiting for me. Ruben's Cabin was brimming with stuff. I stopped off at Humbugs and Merrymakers. Sweets for you Eliza and this is for you,' he said handing Tipp a brown paper bag.

Tip opened it to reveal a thin coloured tube. 'Wow, a kaleidoscope. Thanks.'

'Turn it around,' Huck said, helping himself to one of Eliza's wriggling jelly worms. 'It's a cloud watcher too.'

Tipp turned the other end up towards the approaching night sky.

'What does it do?' asked Eliza.

'It allows us to see the clouds in their true colours – just like a rainbow. When the sun shines on water droplets, we can see all the beautiful colours that make a rainbow. Clouds are full of water too, so when the sun shines and we look through this telescope, we can see these magical colours as well,' Tipp explained as Eliza took a turn to look through it.

'Merrymakers is always fun,' said Huck. 'Ruben's Cabin was a little creepy though. I didn't actually expect to bump into old sleepy head.'

'I never dared venture in there. I always heard tales of how old and scary Ruben was, if he was ever awake,' said Eliza.

Tipp laughed. 'He *is* old and scary but he also has the most amazing collection of whatnots, collected from all over the world. He even keeps an assortment of clouds in miniature glass bottles.'

They sat for a while, watching coloured clouds roll across the skies over Hobbledown using Tipp's kaleidoscope.

As a gumblegook screeched overhead, Huck brushed the dirt from his trousers. 'Time we left,' he said swinging the satchel onto his back. 'Let's go to the mine and check on Emeralda. If *our* crystallite necklaces have faded, maybe her glow has too.'

The moon cast its light to the dark path as they made their way towards the mine. They came to a clearing full of rocks and metal sluice boxes used for mining. The tin wagon stood empty until the morning when it would once again begin its work carrying crystallite back and forth across Hobbledown. A sign hung beside it.

WELCOME TO HOBBLEDOWN MINE!
Visitors please report to
Professor Topperpot
Tin wagon departs every half hour.

The mines are at the heart of Hobbledown and Hobblers came from all over the world, even as far as Clacktonia, to dig and learn about mining.

'It's very quiet about,' said Tipp looking around rather nervously. 'Everyone must be at the meeting.'

'Don't worry, we'll only be a minute or so,' replied Huck as he led the way down several stone steps to a chamber where wooden doors, of various sizes, lined the stone walls; doors now locked up for the night.

'Even the miners have finished early. Only us down here in the dark,' Tipp whispered to Eliza. 'Kind of creepy at night.'

'All this talk of glime has given you the

jitters,' said Eliza giving him a hug. 'We'll soon be out of here.'

They moved through to another chamber, warmer and lighter than the last where a warm comforting glow filled the room. Hanging just above their heads was a large piece of green crystallite, a gem that shimmered brighter than all the stars in the night sky.

Eliza ran her hands over the stone's smooth surface. 'Emeralda Crystallite. She hasn't faded at all. A perfect piece of crystallite.'

'Truly perfect,' whispered Tipp.

'To think crystallite has been mined for

thousands and thousands of years. I wonder when Emeralda first came here?' wondered Eliza, sitting down beside Huck.

'The Book of Thingamajigs and Whatnots must be able to tell us,' said Huck, pulling out the book from his backpack. Tearing off the brown wrapping paper, he skimmed through the pages. 'Here we are...'

'Seekers, as they are known, look for small, green stones – crystallite, first excavated many years ago by the ancient Egyptians and known for their healing powers. Ancient Hobblers first discovered the Emeralda stone centuries ago whilst mining deep in Potenesia.

It is the largest piece of crystallite ever found and has been in the heart of Hobbledown for over a thousand moons. A precious stone with the power to heal, it will provide a natural barrier – to protect and to hold safely whatever is placed within its luminous care.

It is the strongest of all precious stones and it will change colour if the animals are feeling happy or sad. The Hobbler's have mined crystallite for centuries and its strength is considered important to a Hobblers way of life.'

'No wonder we still seek for it,' said Tipp. 'It's very powerful. Fern had to deal with an injured gumblegook the other day and her necklace turned bright red. Talking of Fern, has anyone seen her yet?'

Eliza frowned. 'No, I haven't. It's unusual for her not to tell us if she was going somewhere.'

'I think we should mention it to the Professor,' said Huck. 'Come on, we don't want to be late.'

Several metal tins jangled in the breeze as the Hobblers climbed out of the mine, and walked alongside the Rickety Rack, a small hut where the crystallite supply was stored. Something green glimmered in the moonlight. Eliza stopped. 'What's that on the handle?' she asked, reaching out to touch it.

'Careful!' said Huck. 'It looks like whoever left the glime beneath the Quercus Oak has also visited the mine.'

Very slowly, Huck wiped away the glime with his hankie and opened the door. His heart raced as his cowardly friends hid behind him. Taking a deep breath, he stepped inside, overwhelmed by the foul smell that reached his nose, then that familiar twitch and the uncontrollable watering of his eyes.

The Hobblers stood side-by-side and stared. The winter's supply of crystallite had gone. All that remained was a pile of smelly, bubbling glime.

A Startling Discovery

Firmly rooted to the spot they didn't utter a word. Not a single Potenesian word.

There was a tap on the door and into the room shuffled a Hobbler covered in a sludgy coat of leaves and moss with two small eyes that glowed as bright as hot coals.

'Sludgebucket! What are *you* doing here?' asked Huck, clearly surprised to find anyone around so late in the night.

Sludgebucket wiped his face, flicking mud and a rather large worm onto the slimy floor below. He opened his mouth to reveal a toothless grin.

'Should but can't, will but won't, going but staying. Who knows what I should do?'

Huck frowned. Sludgebucket insisted on talking in muddles and it was impossible to understand what he meant.

'The crystallite has gone. All of it,' said Huck shaking his head in disbelief. 'Did *you*

see anyone strange coming into the mine?'

'Hmm ... maybe I didn't or maybe I did? As I was dung burrowing I heard a noise, or a noise heard me. Some scurrying in the bushes but I saw nothing except a pile of green stuff on me noggins.'

Huck scratched his head, quite certain no sense would come of this. None at all.

'Err ... thanks, Sludgebucket ... I think. Are you coming to the meeting?'

'Yes, thanks, I won't,' replied Sludgebucket, scratching his ears then disappearing as quickly as he had arrived, back to the muddy sludgepile he called home.

'This is getting stranger by the minute,' said Huck as they left the Rickety Rack. 'Whoever or *whatever* has stolen the crystallite must be responsible for the glime. Come on, we need to hurry. The Professor doesn't like interruptions.'

As they ran beneath the moonlight, a bomjad bounced across the Hobblers' path, thumping its back legs impatiently as it hurried towards its warm and cosy burrow. Just ahead, bright coloured lanterns hung from the trees and a crackling fire warmed the air. The firebugs danced around the flame-tops, whizzing out of control as their wings sizzled in the heat. (Incredibly foolish creatures and often barred from such events.)

The Hobblers tucked into a feast of oven-baked mallows, mugs of hot chocolate and corn cakes whilst over near the willows and woebegones, the young Hobblers played Bubbleboo! a game involving large bubbles that they could climb inside and roll about in, crying Boo! whenever they bumped into one another.

Huck, Tipp and Eliza arrived just as the Professor stood up ready to begin, his topper hat slanting crookedly upon his head. As Eliza opened her mouth to speak, bursting with news about their earlier discovery, the Professor brought his cane down sharply to the ground. He took the book from Huck urging them to sit quickly and quietly.

Above Hobbledown, the twinkling stars

listened in as a hush fell upon the meeting.

'Welcome,' began the Professor. 'Welcome to the first meeting of this season and it is for a very grave reason that this meeting has been called.'

The Professor leant on his worm-riddled cane and fixed his glasses.

'Glime has been found in Hobbledown,' he continued. 'Very green and *very* sticky, as young Huck found out. It was only through the brave actions of Tipp and Eliza that he finally managed to get out of such a fix. I have heard of strange creatures that live in green bogs, which is why I sent Huck to Potenesia to fetch the Book of Thingamajigs and Whatnots.'

'Erm, Professor? I think...' began Eliza but the Professor simply shushed her as he thumbed through several more pages. His glasses slid to the end of his nose and after several umms and aahs, he carried on. 'It appears that there are several pages here about such creatures.'

He studied one page for several moments

then began to read.

'In a faraway land, beneath the wildest moors is the boggiest bog of Skelactor. For there lurks a creature of the craggiest kind, covered from head to noggin in lime-green slime - with bulging eyes and long dangly arms that drag behind them dripping in slime. Up they will creep 'til they rattle your nose with their foul-smelling stench and pong-breath toes ... beware, beware of a Skibbler!'

Nearby, a grimwoolly bleated and Albert, the alpaca hummed noisily trying to get to sleep. It seemed the animals also sensed that Hobbledown was becoming just a little too peculiar.

Professor Topperpot spun his cane dramatically up into the air.

'Skibblers!' he shouted.

The Hobblers gasped.

The bubbles bumped then booed.

The firebugs fizzled.

They had all read in fairy tales about this creature.

'Are you sure?' asked an elder Hobbler,

swatting away a sizzling firebug.

'I believe so,' said the Professor gravely. 'The bogs of Skelactor seem to be covered in green glime.'

'Glime is what I stepped in, isn't it?' asked Huck.

'Glime is gook, slime and yuck … whatever you want to call it,' said the Professor now looking rather worried.

Eliza decided she could keep quiet no longer.

'Professor, the crystallite has gone … all of it.'

'That's why we were late,' Huck explained. 'We were passing the Rickety Rack and spotted glime on the handle so we thought we had better check. We looked inside but the crystallite supply had disappeared. There was nothing left except glime.'

Into the moonlight

The Hobblers were outraged.

'Shhh. Quiet please,' said the Professor. We must remain calm...'

Professor Topperpot?' interrupted Eliza. 'It's not only the crystallite that has gone missing. Fern hasn't been seen for two days now and ... well we're worried that something may have happened to her.'

The old Hobbler raised his hand. 'Shhh. We must not jump to conclusions although we cannot rule out the possibility that our young fairy may be in trouble. We shall send out a search party to look for her and the crystallite right away,' he said.

Huck, Tipp and Eliza quickly stepped

forward.

'You can count us in,' said Tipp, the others nodding in agreement.

The Professor smiled. 'Fern is very lucky to have such caring and loyal friends.'

More Hobblers stood up eager to offer their services. 'Excellent,' said the Professor. 'Now, remember to check the barns and burrows around the fields. She could have fallen anywhere. Good luck, Hobblers.'

Carrying sticks and lanterns, the search parties began to look all over Hobbledown.

'No-one knows their way around here better than Fern. I believe the Skibblers have *everything* to do with her disappearance,' said Eliza crossly as they checked out the brayers now fast asleep on the hay. Gulliver rattled his teeth beside Artemis, who swished his tail back and forth, shooing away a troublesome creepy-crawly.

'I think you're right, Eliza,' said Huck gloomily. He hated being out in the dark of the night with creepy Skibblers about. He wanted to

be back in his cosy home like the Hobbledown animals that were now fast asleep.

From the distance, they heard the merry tune of one other Hobbler who was also wide-awake.

'Treasure I not have?

Oh, I have, yes I do!

A bucket of worms, a wheel or two,

plenty of sludging for me to do.

I shall scramble about –

I shall search, I shall find

any clues, any slime that has been left behind.

Digging and finding through the sludge I will,

To seek a goggle, a hat – even a pimpertail quill.'

'Sludgebucket's still dung-burrowing,' said Eliza as she turned over flowerpots and hay bales, 'and his rhymes are as confusing as ever!'

'He never seems to sleep. Day and night he sings ... *all* night sometimes,' said Huck with a grin.

They continued to search through the Willow Field of Confusion, the Willows and

Woebegones – *anywhere* where Fern may have fallen yet they could find no sign of the small Grig fairy.

'This is useless,' said Eliza wearily as they rested. 'If the Skibblers are responsible then we need to track them down first.'

'Track *them* down first? ' Huck asked slowly. 'Why do I not like the sound of that?'

Eliza sighed. 'Come on, Huck. If we go back to the Quercus Oak where the glime was first discovered then maybe we can find something – a clue that will lead us to her.'

'*And* the Skibblers…' Huck mumbled as he followed her towards the tree.

'Ok, let's look around. The Skibblers can't just disappear,' said Eliza, kneeling to inspect the earth in front of her. 'There seems to be lots of Hobbler footprints. These tracks here on the left belong to gumblegooks; I would recognize *their* small prints anywhere. These are a little different though … seems to be several odd-sized tracks,' said Eliza as she ran her hands over a further set of strange markings embedded in the soil. 'Hmmm, I wonder if that's the answer.'

'What?' asked Tipp.

'Just a thought,' she replied. 'Huck, didn't you say your boots had gone missing?'

'Yes. I left them outside after cleaning the snufflers' pen. That's why I'm bootless. Why?'

'If I'm right, and I think I am, it appears that our slimy visitors may have 'borrowed' your boots to try and cover their tracks,' said Eliza, brushing away more leaves to reveal yet another set of marks on the ground. 'Look at these marks just behind each boot print. They may have been clever trying to disguise their trail yet they forgot the scrape marks their trailing arms leave behind.'

Huck and Tipp leant in for a closer look.

'I don't know what's worse. Discovering the trail of Skibblers or the fact that their gooey noggins have been inside my precious boots.' said Huck crossly. 'I waited ages for the cobblers in Potenesia to make them and now I fear I shall never see them again.'

Huck held up his lantern and grumpily led the way, following the tracks that took them through the snufflers' field to the faraway thickets of Hobbledown. As they pushed through the dense undergrowth, they could see small, green blobs glimmering in the moonlight, meaning they were going the right way.

Eliza cried out as she tripped over something in the darkness. Something soft and squishy…

Shadows in the thicket

'**O**uch!' Eliza cried as she picked herself up from the ground clutching two peculiar-sized boots.

Huck grinned. 'My boots,' he said hugging them as though he had found a long lost friend. 'Thanks, Eliza.'

He peered inside, his nose twitching slightly as small traces of glime slithered out of the tops. 'Yuck. Now what do I do with them?'

'Wear them,' said Tipp. 'Otherwise you might get some nasty thorns in your noggins if you're not careful.'

Huck eased them on, shivering as the unmistakable feeling of glime mingled between his noggins once again.

'Ooh … I'm not sure I like this,' he grumbled.

Tipp and Eliza giggled as the boots squelched noisily with every step their friend took. Further and further into the bushes they

went, barely able to see the tracks beneath the twigs and leaves.

As they rested in the nook of a gumblegook tree, a waft of burning willow and popping acorns floated underneath their noses.

'Can you smell that?' asked Tipp leaning out to take a better look.

'Shhh,' said Eliza urgently, pulling her friends back into the tree. 'Over there. Look at those shadows leaping about!'

The three Hobblers peered into the darkness. Through the trees, around a fire, danced the ugliest creatures they had ever seen.

'Skibblers,' whispered Eliza, hardly daring to breathe. They were skinny with bulging eyes that popped out from beneath tufts of braided hair. Their ears were even bigger than a brayers with arms that trailed all the way down to the ground. On top of a pile of spears sat a Skibbler, tapping on a drum whilst the other strange creatures sang very softly. A song that sent goosebumps cursing over the watching

Hobblers.

'From the deep, dark bogs of Skelactor,
we come to knock on the Hobbler's door.
With a plan so clever, a plan so fine,
Leaving behind us a trail of slime.
A treasure we seek of the greatest kind
For most cunning are Skibblers and we will
search till we find
this magical treasure, with its secrets of old
and then our true quest will slowly unfold...'

From a hole in the ground, a Skibbler climbed up into the clearing, covering it back over with bracken and leaves.

'So that's where they came from. They must have burrowed underground all the way from Skelactor. Horrible, frightful creatures,' said Huck hiding as far inside the tree as he possibly could. He had no plans to be their 'surprise' guest for campfire songs.

'Fern could be in there ... with them.' whispered Eliza worriedly. 'Yet, now we've actually found them, I don't know what to do. I didn't expect so many of them and with only

three of us. I guess we should have waited with the others.'

Huck crept slowly out of the hollow.

'Old Pip mentioned that Ruben heard a scratching and tapping sound beneath the ground several days ago. I bet it was the Skibblers. At least we found their camp, Eliza. Let's hurry back and tell the Professor. He'll know what to do.'

The Hobblers ran back towards Hobbledown, leaving behind the strange sight they had discovered in the woods. Professor Topperpot sat with the two other search parties, sipping at warm rosehip tea.

'We were just planning to send a search party out to find you three. By the look on your faces I take it you have had quite an adventure,' said the Professor.

'We saw the Skibblers!' said Eliza breathlessly.

'Loads of them,' added Tipp. 'They were dancing and singing around a fire. Real creepy looking things.'

'And Fern? Any sign of her?' asked an elder.

Huck shook his head. 'It was too dangerous to try and get any closer. Skibblers are *not* the type of creatures to pop in and have tea with! They were telling a tale about stealing into Hobbledown whenever they like.'

'Were they now?' asked the Professor twiddling with his moustache, a twinkle in his old grey eyes. 'I think tea with these chaps sounds like a mighty fine idea, Huck. And I know just the perfect guest who can introduce us.'

A Grand Plan and a little piece of pie

The next morning Hobbledown prepared for battle. After a night of careful planning, attack on the enemy would commence at dusk and everyone needed to help.

Eliza stood quietly beneath the Quercus looking up at Fern's empty home. 'I hope she's alright. Do you think the Skibblers have captured her?' Eliza asked sadly.

'We'll find her, wherever she is. Let's try not to worry,' replied Huck, chipping away at a thin wooden spear.

Tipp hammered upon a flat piece of metal. 'What do you think of my shield?' he asked. 'Not a single Skibbler can glime me with this for protection.'

A group of elder Hobbler women chattered excitedly as they sewed prickles and thistles onto battle tunics, whilst the men sharpened long sticks, perfect for prodding troublesome Skibblers.

Golden pheasant feathers were attached to tin hats along with pinecones and acorns.

Mud was smeared across faces and leaves tucked into their clothing. It would be hard for anyone to spot them amongst the trees and bushes.

Down in the mine the remaining crystallite was loaded onto the tin wagon and taken up to the Copse, where it was placed along the ground to form a pathway – a crystallite pathway that would let Rumpletump stomp in one direction only ... all the way to the Skibblers camp. The power of the precious crystals would ensure that he could not stomp anywhere else in Hobbledown.

The Skibblers were not expecting visitors and they were absolutely and most definitely not expecting a twenty noggins long Rumpletump.

The Hobbler army gathered by the Copse, preparing for the biggest battle they would ever face. Huck and Eliza stood next to Sludgebucket, who had an old metal pot upon his head and a frying pan in his hand, ready to battle any troublesome Skibbler. With spears at the ready, shields held high and their hearts full of Hobbler courage they awaited the signal.

'Ready, Hobblers?' Professor Topperpot lifted his cane high into the air. 'To battle!' he cried.

'To battle!' the Hobblers replied.

A Hobbler ran forward and removed the remaining crystal, placing it where the pathway began. Then they waited for that oh-so-familiar sound.

Swish, swish, swish.

Tipp hurried forward and put a piece of pie down upon the ground. He then ran along the pathway until he reached the edge of the thicket where he placed another oozing piece, perfect bait for a roaming Rumpletump.

Stomp, stomp, stomp.

The beast suddenly appeared near the entrance, his nostrils flaring as he smelt intruders. The Hobblers trembled as he moved towards them – his giant claws squashing everything beneath as a frightened field mouse dived for cover. He sniffed the air hungrily.

Sniff, Sniff, Sniff.

The Hobblers quickly realised he was only interested in the sweet smell of Tipp's custard pie.

With one great **chomp**, he gobbled it up, looking hungrily around for the next.

He then began stomping down the path with his long tail swaying behind him. Huck covered his mouth trying to rid himself of the hiccups that were trying to escape.

'Shhh.' said Eliza.

'I can't help it,' said Huck helplessly as he shook then jumped.

'Try harder,' demanded Eliza. Huck grabbed his hankie, muffling every escaping sound as they marched behind Rumpletump all the way across Hobbledown to the edge of the thicket.

They stopped when Rumpletump stopped, moved when Rumpletump moved, through brambles and bushes, along past the gumblegook trees until the smell of smoke drifted under their noses and they knew they were there, at the Skibblers' camp.

Tea with the Skibblers

Rumpletump stomped ahead. The Hobblers raised their shields in front of them, gripping their wooden spears firmly, tips pointed forward. On the front line stood Huck, Tipp, Sludgebucket and the miners, only their shaking legs betraying their bravery. Just behind was Eliza, fiddling nervously with her feathered armour as like the rest of the Hobbler army, she prepared to face these peculiar creatures.

Not a leaf rustled nor an animal stirred. Only the Skibblers whispered and gibbered. With their misshapen ears and large hooked noses, set amongst greedy eyes, they peered eagerly at their chief, who was now etching markings on the ground.

'Looks like they're making plans,' whispered Eliza, edging slowly forward. 'Plans to steal from us again!'

'Well this time they won't get the chance,' said Tipp, pulling out more pie from his bag.

'Ok, Rumpletump. The pathway stops here. Let's see if Professor Topperpot's plan works.'

Tipp hurled the pie as hard as he could, pop-bang into the middle of the crackling fire. Rumpletump, happily scratching his back against a silver birch, stopped and looked around. His eyes narrowed and his nostrils flared as he stomped closer towards the fire – a fire where a tasty treat awaited in the flames. 'That's it,' said Tipp softly. 'Nice and gently …

just a little bit more. '

Rumpletump's eyes began to water and his nose began to twitch as he moved right behind the scheming Skibblers.

'Oh no, Chief Cockalorum! A beast, a beast, oh globbero!' the creatures cried as they turned to find themselves not only facing a beast, but also an army of angry Hobblers.

Drool slithered from Rumpletump's mighty jaws. The Skibblers' eyes grew bigger and bigger,

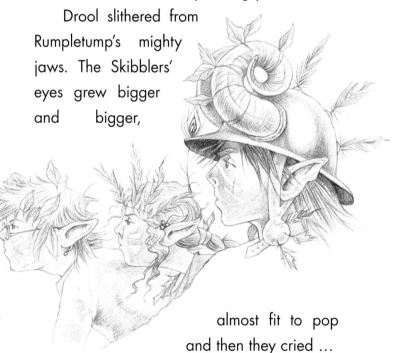

almost fit to pop and then they cried …

'A beast, a beast –
Oh no, no, no!
We must stay and fight,
in the dark of night.
A guest we've not planned
What shall we do?
A beast, a beast
Oh what a fright!'

'To battle!' cried the Hobblers and with that, they charged into the middle of the Skibblers' camp right behind Rumpletump seeking his pie.

'Globbero!' crowed the Skibblers raising their spears in defence, a fearsome gaggle of at least two dozen. The battle began, one that every Hobbler would remember forever.

Spear clashed against spear. Howls and yelps rang out around the woodland as sharp points jabbed at the Skibblers. Huck, Tipp, and a group of younger Hobblers, all skilled wood fighters, advanced courageously, knowing now was the only chance they had if they were to rid Hobbledown of these unwanted visitors. The Skibblers gnashed their rotten teeth in fury as they tried to defend themselves, their spears meeting with the strong metal of the Hobblers' shields. The Hobblers, however, remained calm and strong as the battle raged on.

'There's not many left,' said Eliza looking around as Rumpletump held a Skibbler in between his two front teeth, and then dropped the howling creature straight down the hole!

'Look at Rumpletump. He is doing a great job rounding them up. He would be brilliant with the grimwoollies,' said Tipp in astonishment. 'Some of our elders are growing tired so I guess it's up to us to make sure we get rid of this last handful.'

'Sludgebucket is working hard too,' said Eliza, as her sludgy friend, frying pan firmly in one hand and saucepan in the other, chased after several frightened Skibblers bopping them firmly upon their heads.

'To the hole you go to say goodbye or bye for good,' said Sludgebucket narrowly avoiding an air-borne spear flying towards him.

Up on a moss-covered rock, a Skibbler removed a catapult from his belt and with a cry of globbero! fired a ball of glime straight at Rumpletump's behind.

'Chief Cockalorum?' gibbered a Skibbler standing beside the bandana-clad creature. 'I'm not sure that was a good idea.'

'Globberish! Globberish and nonsense!' cried Cockalorum. 'Skibblers afraid of nothing.' Rumpletump grunted, burped, and then opened his ever-so-scary jaws to reveal the sharpest teeth this foolish Skibbler had ever, ever seen. The Skibbler's eyes narrowed as he placed his spear onto the ground, smiling sweetly at the beast in front of him. (Do remember that Skibblers cannot be charming, however hard they try.) With a skip then a scuttle, he dashed towards the hole in the ground. The smile quickly turned to a grimace as Cockalorum loaded his catapult once more, and fired a final ball of glime, splat onto Rumpletump's nose.

'That should do it!' whispered Huck,

placing a well-executed jab to an approaching Skibbler's toe. 'Now he'll be really cross!'

The Hobblers could only stare as a stampeding Rumpletump chased Cockalorum around the fire, snapping at the noggins of the howling Skibbler.

'Ouch, globber! – oh, ouch,' cried Cockalorum, leaping over a log desperate to rid himself of the beast. With a final battle cry, he jumped across Rumpletump's tail and bolted straight down the hole that would take him back to the dreadful bogs he had first come from.

As Cockalorum disappeared, his long bony fingers wrapped themselves around the muddy noggin belonging to Sludgebucket, tugging the poor Hobbler straight down into the deepest pits of the earth.

'Sludgebucket!' cried Eliza. Panic-stricken she ran to the hole, sinking to her knees, not caring that Rumpletump was only several stomps behind her. 'Oh no. Huck! What can we do?'

The Hobblers dropped their spears, leaving the remaining Skibbler under the watchful and hungry eye of Rumpletump and hurried over to join Eliza.

'He's gone,' sobbed Eliza kneeling down, 'with his funny riddles and…'

'Shhh!' said Huck as he peered into the bottomless pit. 'Can you hear that?'

They could hear something scrabbling about, a soft humming somewhere in the distance. Amongst the darkness appeared a light steadily growing brighter and brighter. As it moved closer towards them, they could see two glowing eyes and a toothy grin.

'Sludgebucket!' cried Eliza happily, helping Huck heave him up onto the dry ground. 'We thought we had lost you.'

'Sludgebucket loves a good muddy hole … no … yes! Oh yes I do.' he grinned, scraping away a clump of squelchy mud from his hat. 'Skibblers gone but what a mess – need to rest.'

Not caring about the sludge, Eliza gave him a firm squeeze. Sludgebucket belonged only in Hobbledown and she was very relieved to have him back.

'Let's finish this off,' said Huck as he straightened his battle hat and marched with the Hobblers back into the clearing. 'Ready?'

Tipp nodded. He blew sharply on his whistle and threw the last piece of pie as far along the crystallite path as he could. With a final grunt, Rumpletump dashed along the path after the pie and home to the Copse.

'Perfect,' said Huck. 'Sludgebucket … pull that log over the hole to block it whilst we bag this Skibbler up.'

With much poking and prodding, the Skibbler was bundled into a sack and fastened tightly with a rope. The Hobblers stood together, victorious, the remains of burning wood and broken spears left scattered around the clearing. With their aching bodies and torn clothing, they helped the weary elders back to Hobbledown.

'That was quite a night! Rumpletump did exactly as we hoped, and more. With this one remaining Skibbler we can hopefully find out where Fern is,' said Eliza happily. 'Are you ok, Huck?'

'I've been in worse fixes I guess,' he grinned as glime slid down the horns on his hat. 'Horrible creatures! They steal what they like – treasures like crystallite, shiny objects, my gumboots and even poor Fern.'

'Well this one is certainly a lively bag of trouble,' she said, helping Huck carry the shaking sack into Hobbledown. Tipp was already excitedly relaying details of the entire battle to Professor Topperpot who was looking very relieved to find them all safe and well.

'Well done! It appears that the Skibblers received quite a shock, as I had hoped. Let us hope they never return to Hobbledown although they were very eager to come all this way just for a little treasure. Quite peculiar creatures I must say. It is almost as if…' Professor Topperpot stopped.

'As if what Professor?' asked Eliza dropping the heavy sack by his noggins.

'Nothing, my dear, nothing I'm sure,'

he replied thoughtfully. 'Now, where is this creature? I am quite curious to see what one looks like.'

Huck removed the cord from around the wheat sack.

'Globberish, globberish,' spluttered the squashed up Skibbler as it rolled out onto the ground. 'Globb, globb, globb...' it choked.

'Enough!' said the Professor. 'Foolish creature. Now, where is our crystallite?'

'Smidge got nothing to say. Cockalorum

will go globbero if I tell you,' said Smidge, his eyes rolling around and about.

'Not as 'globbero' as Rumpletump, if I bring *him* over to say hello,' warned the Professor.

'Oh no, no, no, the beast? Follow me, follow me…' said Smidge as he quickly led the way towards the Quercus Oak and to the spot where Huck had first discovered the glime. Kneeling down, Smidge began to scrabble away at the earth to reveal a deep hollow hidden in the roots. There, in front of their very eyes, was the crystallite, shimmering as brightly as ever although covered in glime.

'Well I never,' said the Professor. 'It was here under our noses the whole time. Who would have thought? The glime must have weakened the crystallite causing our crystals to weaken. But why would they keep it here, in Hobbledown?'

Huck kept his spear close to Smidge just in case he tried any tricks.

Eliza stepped forward. 'It does seem strange but now we have the crystallite back what about Fern? Where have you taken her, Smidge?' she demanded standing face to face with the slimy green creature.

'Globberish! Know nothing about a fairy,' said the Skibbler.

'See,' cried Eliza angrily. 'I never said she was a fairy. He is fibbing … he does know.'

Smidge fiddled nervously with the feather in his hair. Even the mention of sending him to Endlesdom did not do any good, and if you were ever sent to the darkest, gloomiest pits of Endlesdom, then it would be a sorry trip indeed.

'Let us keep him somewhere safe, maybe near Rumpletump, where he will hopefully come to his senses, although I strongly doubt he has any! Maybe after a few stomps from Rumpletump, he will tell us exactly where Fern is,' chuckled the Professor.

Merry-down day

Pastel pink and powder blue clouds floated over a peaceful Hobbledown. The bobillies bleated noisily as they clip-clopped over wooden steps, enjoying the warmth of the morning sun. Gertrude fussed contentedly with the baby snufflers nuzzling beneath her, eager for their breakfast. The animals were much happier now that the crystallite was back in place and harmony had returned.

Every trace of glime had been cleaned away and bright coloured flags were hoisted high, ready for Merrydown day. A day of dancing, music, puppet shows and feasts.

'Merrydown in Hobbledown,' sang a Hobbler as he juggled a jumble of balls to the oohs and aahs of the awestruck Hobbler children. Over in the fields the grimwoollies prepared for a race as the watching gumblegooks flocked above, cackling louder than ever. Barrels were full of apples and buttered corn, and tables groaned beneath the weight of fresh scones, genoose syrup and fresh strawberries, buttered sweet corn and of course, Tipp's custard pies.

Visitors from far and wide had come to join in the merriment – Mr Humbug, Mr Merrymaker, Old Pip, who Eliza agreed was very, *very* old indeed and a half-asleep Ruben. It was even rumoured that the Pogwips from

Nonsuch would be attending.

Beneath the Quercus, a quartet struck up a tune on their fiddles as the younger ones danced in and out of the trailing willow leaves waiting for the puppet show to begin, the story of the Hobbler Cobblers and the Lantern Thief.

Sludgebucket, joined in with the fiddlers, happily banging upon his tin pot singing …

'Merrydown, diddle down
what a day, what a day.
The Skibblers have gone far away, far away.
Never here to return
merry ho - merry heigh.'

Tipp and Huck clapped along, watching Eliza pour a bucketful of red and green apples into Gertrude's trough. All three of them wore hats, adorned with feathers of every kind, a must if they were to join in with the parade later that day.

'Another search party has just gone out,' said Huck as he fixed a black feather into his hat.

Eliza wiped her hands and came to sit beside them. 'I've searched high and low. Those pesky creatures have hidden her well, just like they did with the crystallite, but where?'

'Magpies, that's what they're like. Stealing treasures and whatnots. Probably explains why they covered themselves in pimpertail feathers. That Smidge had one tucked in his hair just like you, Eliza.'

Eliza dropped the bucket she was holding and stood silent for a moment, her freckled face a mixture of frowns and thoughts.

'That's it!' she cried. Huck and Tipp hurried behind her as she headed towards Porello's roost.

'What's going on?' asked Huck.

'You'll see,' said Eliza as she slowly crept past the pimpertail, who was pecking at seeds on the ground. 'Porello's been really grumpy for days now. I couldn't understand why but just now you said something that suddenly made me wonder...'

Eliza opened the door to Porello's rather

unusual roost and felt around the straw until she touched something soft – something that wriggled.

A cloth pouch. Quickly, she pulled open the drawstrings and a golden spark shot out into the air.

'Fern!' said Eliza delightedly. 'We have looked *everywhere* for you.'

The small fairy spun around and flew to the top of a gumblegook tree then back down again to land in the palm of Eliza's hand. Fern's large violet eyes shimmered with excitement as she flapped her wings, happy to be free.

Eliza tickled the fairy's chin playfully. 'We missed you. You wouldn't believe the trouble we've had over the past few days.'

Fern placed her hands on her hips and frowned. 'The trouble *you've* had?' began the fairy crossly. 'Why, if I ever get my hands on one of those long-haired, glimy creatures.'

She let off another spark of gold dust. Huck and Tipp moved aside as a crowd of Hobblers and Professor Topperpot soon arrived; the news of Fern's discovery had already spread across Hobbledown.

'Welcome back, Fern. You gave us quite a worry, especially your three friends here,' said the Professor wearing a bowler hat covered in gumblegook feathers.

Huck, Tipp and Eliza grinned. Fern blushed brighter than her red cap.

'I didn't go anywhere, Professor. I was right here, stuck in that pouch with Porello nesting on top of me. He was *not* happy at all,' said Fern, 'and neither was I. As I was hanging out my washing, I heard a noise below the Quercus. I crept down to take a look and there below were the strangest creatures I had ever seen, digging a deep hole in the ground,' she said pulling a pimpertail feather from out of her hair. 'One of them was talking about stealing the crystallite and what a clever plan it was.'

'Did he now?' the Professor asked rubbing his whiskers thoughtfully. 'Can you remember what else he said?'

'Well, he mentioned something about how it would only be a clever plan *if* it meant you went to Potenesia to fetch the Book of Thingamajigs and Whatsa ... something.'

'Whatnots?' said Eliza.

'That's the one. They said you wouldn't like things getting too mysterical and it would be in your nature to go and fetch the book to find out more.'

'Quite right,' muttered Huck.

'Once they saw me and realised I'd heard everything, they threw this yucky green stuff at me and then grabbed me. I had just enough time to raise the flag, hoping you would come and visit, as you always do when it's baking day,' she said smiling at Huck.

'I *always* visit on baking day,' laughed Huck patting his stomach.

'Cockalorum told them to put me somewhere safe where I couldn't tell anyone about their secrets. They were dreadful looking creatures,' said Fern with a shiver.

'Bulgy eyes and dripping with green glime?' Huck asked.

'Yes. How did *you* know that?'

'It's a long story, Fern. A story that will go down as the greatest battle Hobbledown has ever faced,' Huck said proudly.

'And one that is almost finished, once we send *this* gibbering fellow back to where he came from,' said the Professor as two Hobblers, with sharp sticks, arrived with Smidge. 'Well, well, Smidge. It seems your fondness for feathers gave the secret away. Cockalorum is not going to be pleased with you. I am now quite happy to send you back but I also require you to take along a simple message. If I ever, ever see a trail of glime, even the smallest spot, then I will send Rumpletump to pay you all a visit!'

'Three cheers for Hobbledown,' cried an elder as the Skibbler was marched off towards the woods and to the troublesome hole in the ground, 'and a cheer for Merrydown day. Let the celebrations *really* begin.

'Hip-hip hooray,' cried the Hobblers as the fiddlers struck up their tune once more.

'Right, now let's join in with the fun,' Eliza said happily, kicking up her heels as she joined in with the dancing. Round and round she spun, her noggins skipping this way and that to the merry sound of the fiddlers.

'The girls are having fun,' said Tipp sitting

beside Huck enjoying marshmallow sticks. 'I'm glad things are less mysterical. That was quite an adventure.'

'It sure was,' replied Huck. 'I've had enough excitement to last me a very long time. In fact, I may even pop in to see Rumpletump later and give him a piece of pie. I think he deserves it.'

'Yes,' said Tipp. 'Rumpletump really did save the day. Come on. Let's Merrydown too.'

Only one Hobbler didn't join in with the merriment or stop to sip a drop of elderflower wine. Only one Hobbler ran as fast as his old legs would carry him until he reached his small home in the heart of Hobbledown. Inside was a room full of books, chairs, boxes and cupboards and a single chest of wooden drawers.

He reached up and pulled open the top drawer.

Professor Topperpot gasped.

The Book of Thingamajigs and Whatnots had gone and all that remained was a tiny spot of glime.

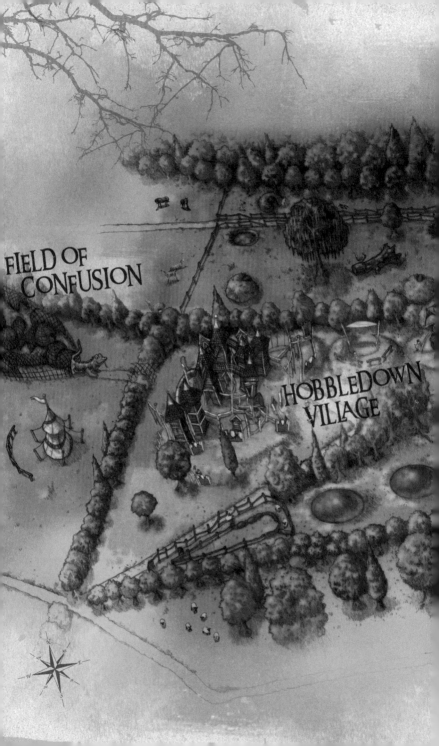

FIELD OF CONFUSION

HOBBLEDOWN VILLAGE